Fashion Trends, Deadly Ends

Brianna Malotke

GREEN AVENUE BOOKS & PUBLISHING LLC

Book designed by Green Avenue Books & Publishing LLC

First Edition Printing

Print ISBN: 9781088018026

EBook ISBN: 9781088018125

From Head to Toe

I'm dedicating this collection to my mom, Rachel McLaughlin, as an apology for "always" killing the mother off in so many of my horror pieces.

Hopefully, this makes you smile.

A huge thank you to Marie and Chris for the support and constant excitement you've both shown me at every step of the way. What started out as a little post–it note with "Write Spooky Stories" scribbled on it has finally turned into a book - and I can't imagine having done it without you guys.

Fashion Trends, Deadly Ends

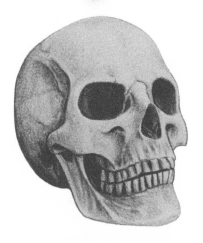

A COLLECTION OF HORROR POETRY
INSPIRED BY HISTORICAL FASHION TRENDS.

BRIANNA MALOTKE

Preface

It doesn't all lead back to devouring "Scary Stories to Tell in the Dark," by Alvin Schwartz, but my love of horror and the macabre definitely grew after reading those books in elementary school. Growing up I loved monster movies, scary stories, and everything about Halloween. Along with these interests, I also loved clothing and costumes. Which is how I ended up pursuing apparel and costume design in college.

In college, I amassed this whole assortment of "fun facts" from studying and researching for different projects. But it wasn't until I took a corsetry class at the London College of Fashion that I realized just how chaotic and deadly fashion was during various time periods. While studying abroad I took advantage of the libraries and took a deep dive into researching the topics I didn't have the time or resources for back at Purdue University.

One of my favorite things about costume design is all of the research that can go into designing pieces for a show. In my personal time, I do read a lot of costume and apparel books, but I get a little more into it when researching for a specific show where I'm designing costumes. During the pandemic, all of my scheduled plays and musicals were canceled. With all of this new time on my hands, I decided to go back to creating spooky stories and poems for fun. As I was thinking about how great having my own poetry collection would be, I realized I could blend my two loves - horror and fashion history.

This poetry collection is inspired by deadly fashion trends. Think poisonous dyes, rib removal for smaller waists, flammable fabric, and more! It only scratches the surface of fashion history, but I hope it inspires and intrigues you to want to learn.

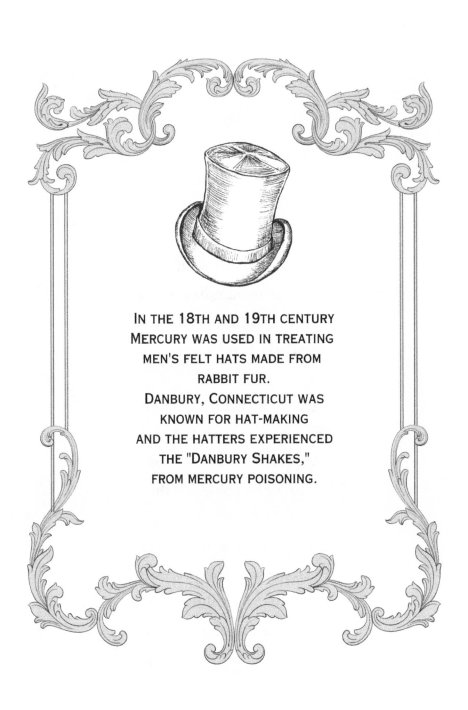

IN THE 18TH AND 19TH CENTURY
MERCURY WAS USED IN TREATING
MEN'S FELT HATS MADE FROM
RABBIT FUR.
DANBURY, CONNECTICUT WAS
KNOWN FOR HAT-MAKING
AND THE HATTERS EXPERIENCED
THE "DANBURY SHAKES,"
FROM MERCURY POISONING.

Containing Danbury Shakes

All throughout town, known
For its hat-making and its fur,
Where the Still River flowed,
People flocked for the creations.

Twiddling along day after day,
The hat makers worked, and
Were consequently exposed,
The mercury seeping into them.

Through the dust and vapors
From the carroting process,
And from the brushing of felt
To secure the fur and the shape.

They began to change, to shake,
Their hands no longer steady,
Their minds no longer strong,
The hatmakers were going mad.

Any man who wanted a tasteful
And polished felt hat, came to
Danbury for their selection,
Though the hatters irritable.

Hats went in and out of style,
Though for those mad hatters
In Danbury, who got the shakes,
The effects were permanent.

Shake Me Down Death

These vibrations shake me to the core
It seems as if my soul is trembling on
Yet I continue work, more and more

Making hats all day long, time long gone
Until my fingers are weak and my mind
More paranoid, I'll sleep until dawn

The next day arrives, I feel blind
From the shaking, my head unsteady now
As my hands shake, the hats well-defined

Made from rabbit, I silently vow
I close my eyes and I whisper out loud
For when Death comes for me, I won't bow

To him or show fear, he'll need be proud
Of my hats and my work and of my strength
Death will need to speak my name aloud

To wake me from this life, as my mind
Wanders - *I'm fearful now* - and he'll need to
Shake me down, before he takes me blind.

Uneasy Now

Shifting from one foot to
The other - uneasy - as
I wait for the gentleman
To make his purchase.

Trembling, trying to hide
As my hands can't control
Themselves, worried about
Everything and anything.

I work all day on these hats,
These magnificent creations
For which I garner society's
Affection, but I am uneasy.

No longer smiling, my teeth
Hidden, my hands, though
They tremble and shake, nails
Tinted with green, I'm uneasy.

Sitting alone in my shop, my
Lovely fur hats surrounding me,
And as I stare intently, I feel
Watched - uneasy - maybe.

Mad as a hatter they whisper,
My shaking more noticeable,
And my smile wicked now,
And they lock me away,
My hats are all alone now.

Madness Creeps Over the Hatter

We're all mad here, they whisper to the empty
Room, to themselves, the air cold and stale
In this padded cell they now call their home.
Their hands calloused, rough from the years
They spent making hats for the wealthy.

Their skin used to the steam and the chemicals
In curing, molding, and sewing the felt pieces
To create the lovely, elaborate, pieces donned
By all those who were well-to-do in high society.

But here they sat, all alone, whispering to no
One, that they're all mad here, the comforting
Tale slipping off their tongue, their eyesight
Distorted as the walls and days blur together,
Time passing them by, we're all mad here.

Whispers fall on lonely ears, clutching their
Palms together, the shaking, the trembling
Normal enough now, we're all mad here, eyes
Closed now - *all mad here* - they whisper.

Soon enough they'll slip into a deep sleep,
Murmuring we're all mad here, on repeat,
Before that eternal slumber creeps, the poor,
Mad hatter who slowly lost their mind,
Though never their passion, dies all alone.

No One is Mad Here

Hands steady, he works all day long
until his eyes grow weary and tired
and his hands ache from making hats.

All of the high–class ladies demand
their hats be made with real fur,
everything must be in this season.

His days are long, working tirelessly
on the numerous new orders placed,
his hands trembling periodically.

Months and months go by, his tremble
now dictating his pace, he's behind
and his mind wanders, his work delayed.

His thoughts are scattered, memories
lost and words misplaced, his beloved
shop is closing for all his work has stopped.

He sits alone now, his tremble permanent,
they watch over him here, listening to his
stories, pitying this poor forgotten mad hatter.

DURING THE LATE 17TH CENTURY
WOMEN WOULD SOMETIMES CATCH
FIRE DUE TO THE SIZE OF THE
HEADDRESS, RESULTING IN
SEVERE BURNS AND
POSSIBLE DEATH.

Crown of Pins

Using delicate, tiny pins,
They weaved her hair - in
and out - with lace and
Ribbons, and even more
Pins to get the ever coveted
And ever stunning height
Of her headdress, and her
Fontange was all the rage
In court, each other lady
Full of sophistication and
Jealousy, as they tried
And failed to duplicate
The elegant look - and
dramatic - height she had
Achieved over and over
Again, though everything

Wonderful comes to an end,
One late evening, arriving
Home from a ball with a
Stomach full of wine and
A heavy head, she went to
Bed without undressing or
Even undoing her hair, and
Made a grave mistake for
She had also not blown out
Any of her candles, and as
She tossed and turned in
Bed, her waking moments
Soon became worse than
Any nightmare she had ever
Experienced, as the heat and
Smoke filled her room, pain
Spread through her every fiber
Of her being, soon the entire
Room was engulfed in flames,
And as her fontange melted
Down, her skin peeled and
Embers cling to what was
Left of her beautiful figure,
When they put the fire out,
A pile of pins was found

Above her skull, a crown
No one would ever want.

Pinned to Remember

Only the best lace, and
The finest ribbons were
Used in her fontange.

Woven in between her
Small cap, her natural hair,
And pinned in place, she
Achieved stunning height.

Popular among all of the
Sophisticated ladies, hers
Was known to be the best.

Larger - and larger - pins
Needed to be used as she
Tried to go higher with her
Fontange, with her status.

Every moment she spent
On her hair seemed to
Yield the desired results.

Looking for more - and
More - status and power
She continued to pursue
A higher, larger, fontange

Fancy ribbon from abroad,
And hand-woven lace with
Larger pins, striving for more.

All it took though was one
Tiny candle, and a step too
Close, for her fontange - in
All its beauty - to catch fire.

Up in the flames the well
Constructed piece went, and
No one could undo it quickly.

Her burns severe, her beauty
Forever gone, though everyone
Was sure to remember the
Lady who went up in smoke.

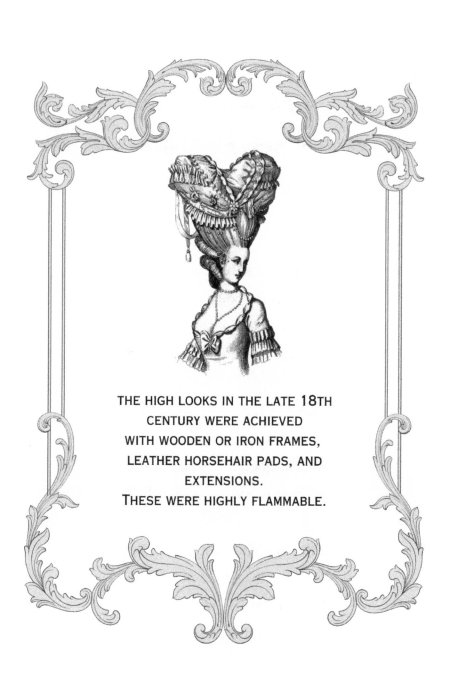

THE HIGH LOOKS IN THE LATE 18TH
CENTURY WERE ACHIEVED
WITH WOODEN OR IRON FRAMES,
LEATHER HORSEHAIR PADS, AND
EXTENSIONS.
THESE WERE HIGHLY FLAMMABLE.

Headdress Blaze

Inspired by the 18th-century print "L'incendie des coiffures".

Exaggerated silhouettes, adorned
with as many bows and as much
lace as she can carry, Eloise
is part of the small elite in society

She's five feet of beauty, but six
If you count her headdress, which
Adds height and dazzles all the
Common people, as she strolls by

At the café with her suitor, she's
Eager to be eye–catching, and
Though she's dainty, her wig is
Hefty, and high, it scrapes the

Base of the chandeliers, the lit
Candles sway slightly as she
Takes small steps, carefully
Moving towards their table

All eyes are on her, for she
Moved just a tad too close,
And while panic overwhelms
Her, her smile never falters

As the flames only grow,
The heat becomes unbearable,
And though they pour water
Over her, the blaze has taken

The toll on her appearance,
Blisters cover her skin, and
She rushed home to recover
No suitor will call now.

The Weight of Society

The weight of her wig,
And the contraption
That supported it, was
Heavy on her head.

Holding her in place,
Both the wig and her
Thoughts, the court and its stern
noblemen too much.

She swayed beneath the
Iron frames attached
To her head, the pads
And extensions woven
About, with everything
Powdered profusely.

She longed for freedom,
For fresh air and minimal
Accessories, but yet she
Was frozen here, someone
Always watching her
Every move, every breath.

Then one day, as if her
Prayers were answered, a
Fire came about, destroying
Everything in its path, climbing
And winding its way through
Each room, she was not spared.

As the flames licked her skin,
Consuming the fibers of her
Silk gown and the wig, as she
Burned she finally felt a taste
Of freedom, the burden of
The heavy wig now gone.

Powdered Without Regret

All the ladies of the court
Wore the finest of silks and
Their delicate bodies were
Draped in shiny jewels and
Doused in fragrant perfumes

Always watching from the dark
Sidelines, she envied
The ladies as they danced, their
Features flawless under the
Candlelight, as they sparkled
And twirled about the ballroom.

She waited until the right
Moment, her wig piled high, its
Shape held with wooden frames
With extensions woven through

Powdered lavishly, her wig
Towered above her tiny
Frame, the crowded ballroom gasped
And hummed praises, her entrance
Would be gossiped about for
Days to come, despite falling
Ill, as she lay bedridden
with a smile on her face and
eyes closed, no regrets to be
had, the lead laced powder too
much for her body, but she'd
be on the mind of the court
forever engrained with them.

IN THE LATE 1800s / EARLY 1900s
THE CELLULOID COMBS USED IN
WOMEN'S HAIR WOULD EXPLODE
WHEN THEY GOT TOO HOT.

Everything Held in Place

Styling her hair, she piled it up high,
Wanting to achieve that fashionable
Look where her curls were perfect
And everything was held in place.

Ivory no longer in fashion, Penelope
Instead used one of the new combs to
Slide some of her unruly red locks
Into place, sweeping them away from
Her face and up into a stylish hairdo.

The weight of her hair, heavy, but
Everything held in place, the comb
Freeing her face from any chance of
A loose strand falling out of place.

Ready for the romantic evening
Ahead of her, Penelope went to the
Restaurant, and sitting at a table
For two, she waited by the fire,
Warming her hands while waiting.

The warmth was lovely, the flames
A beautiful mix of colors, mesmerized
By the roaring fire, she leaned in just
A tad too close, her comb overheating.

The crackling of the fire was dim
Compared to the explosion the comb
Seemed to make, the sound popping,
The fire spreading, her hair sizzling
And smoking, as she tried to put it out.

Hands quickly came to her aid, rolling
Her about, the smell of burnt flesh
Overwhelmed her senses, she closed
Her eyes, her beauty was surely gone.

Caring for My Beard

My grey beard, my main feature,
Is well-maintained, and always
Brushed and oiled and everything
Done just right, for that's how
Society works, if you want a ring.

Tall and lanky, I don't have much
In the ways of appearance, but I do
Have my beard and piercing eyes
That they say looks like an ocean's
Storm, with those I'm a real prize.

The finest garments cannot change
A man, but the facial hair can help,
With these I blend, no longer unique
Smiling, thinking of a life with a wife,
I comb my beard every day, each week.

Long gone are the ornate ivory combs,
Popular celluloid ones are used now,
Brushing, oiling, and styling my beard
Daydreaming of a wonderful wedding
A life full of laughter, oh to be revered.

Looking into the fire, the flames warm
Against my face as I lean closer in,
A popping sound erupts as smoke
Consumes my senses, my comb tucked
In my beard, now melted and broke.

My facial hair, my winning feature,
Singed and uneven, not much to do
Except cut it off and treat the skin
Underneath that blistered and oozed,
One day it'll grow back, and I'll win.

BELLADONNA EYE DROPS
WERE USED TO DILATE THE PUPILS
TO LOOK LIKE A ROMANTIC PAINTING
BUT CAUSED BLURRED VISION
AND POTENTIAL LOSS OF VISION.

Those Belladonna Eyes

She had memorized every inch
Of the Italian painting, the colors
Astounding, the porcelain woman
Staring off to the side, her features
Soft - yet those eyes had heat
and desire - how oh how could she be
Equally seductive in her beauty?

Makeup and perfume could not
Help her, though she tried and
Tried different combinations,
Always trying hopelessly to have
Those alluring eyes, yearning for
Suitors and for true love, she knew
Beauty was the key to happiness.

Finally, the solution came, and with
The eye drops she had achieved the
Look she had so desired, her pupils
Dilated, and paired with everything
Else she had the full package, despite
The lingering effects, she knew her
Appearance was flawless, heavenly.

Through squinted eyes, she tried her
Best to remain in high society, the
Sun too bright, many days now spent
In the drawing–room, where she knew
The location of every item, her vision
Now blurred - everything just a little
bit hazy - but still, she was beautiful.

Luckily, she had long ago memorized
Her favorite painting, her eyes were
Now too weary - but the drops had
done wonders - she knew one day
Her vision would go but for now she
Would celebrate, for she had a lovely
Home, husband, and Belladonna eyes.

Just a Few Drops

Wide-eyed beauty, clad in the best
Satin and silks of the most flattering
Colors and styles for your figure,
You want more, you crave it all.

Lusting after the handsome suitor,
He's courting all of the eligible ladies
This season, and you want to make
A lasting impression, you want him.

Your choices were dire, the belladonna
Drops easily obtainable, all the young
Ladies desire romance, their rosy
Cheeks and lips like a work of art.

With blurry eyes, you chose your
Path - you dug your grave - all for
A man's hand, pushed by your desire
And search for beauty in society's eyes.

You wallow, your throat hoarse, as
You pass your days all alone with the
Curtains drawn, the sunlight much
Too bright, your cries are faint now.

Wide-eyed beauty, clad in the best
Satin and silks, you sit wilting just
Like a single pulled rose, the colors
Faded and dim, just your eyesight.

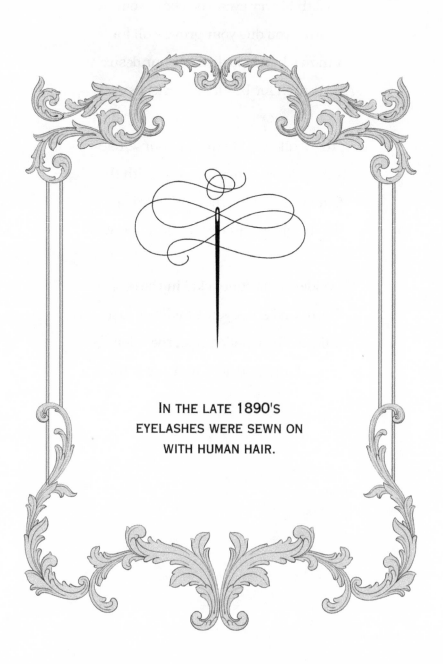

IN THE LATE 1890'S
EYELASHES WERE SEWN ON
WITH HUMAN HAIR.

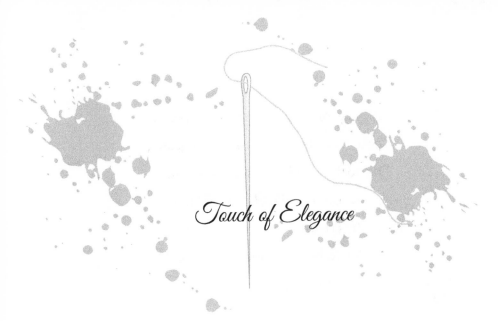

Touch of Elegance

The stitches, ever so small, were
Made slowly by steady hands,
But that didn't mean the long
Awaited procedure was lacking
Pain, it hurt so much she could
Barely hold in the screams that
Desperately wanted to escape.

She needed this to go smoothly,
She had it all, except for that final
Touch of elegance.

A glass of whiskey, a bit of rope,
These were her only anesthetics as
The doctor, clad in a suit urged her
To remain calm as he sewed new
Eyelashes from fur perfectly matched
In color to her own lashes, she took
A muffled breath, hoping it was over.

Her delicate features could only
Go so far, she needed this dramatic
Touch of elegance.

Her swollen eyelids ached, her vision
Much too hazy, the doctor's words
Echoed in her head until she could hear
Nothing else, he had made a horrible
mistake - an error with her eye - for
Which he was deeply sorry, so now
Here she was, in pain and only one eye.

Dazzling Eyes

She stared into the mirror, really
Concentrating on the face staring
Back at her, the reflected eyes a
Hazel with flecks of gold mixed
Within, yet not alluring enough.

Her smile was lovely - or so they
all said - with lips soft and supple,
Her reflection smiled at her, with
Eyes blank and lacking something.

It was all the rage, to have dazzling
Eyes, to blink and smile and catch
The attention of a beau, to be the
Belle of any ball, to be luminous.

With determination, and beauty on
Her mind, she set out for the latest
Fashion trend, and without any kind
Of numbing or anesthesia, she did it.

Through pain and tears, she had new
Dazzling lashes, thick and heavy on
Her eyes, the bleeding would stop,
The small stiches hidden in her lids.

She stared into the mirror, through
Hazy glimpses, the lashes oozing,
Everything was a bit clouded, but
Through the small slits of vision,
Her reflection looked beautiful.

Escaping Tears

Thoroughly cleaned, rubbed
With solution, the area now
Sterile and ready for us to
Begin the procedure,
The needle is fine in nature
Tiny and adequate for its
Role in these actions, the
Hair - a perfect match of
Course - is ready as well,
The young girl, so eager to
Please her mother - and
Society as well - is much
Too nervous, with eyes
Tight shut, only a few
Tears escaped thus far,
We wait a few moments,

Letting her calm down,
Then with careful precision
We carry on, running the
Needle through the edges
Of the eyelids, looping
The hair to add that extra
Oomph to her naturally
Short and thin lashes,
Once the swelling subsides
And the chance of any
Infection is gone - along
With her tears - and any
Pain she will be pleased,
They all say beauty is pain
Afterall, and everyone
Wants to feel beautiful.

Skipping this Stitch

with steady hands she takes
a deep breath in – one, two,
three – and out, trying to
relax her mind, her hand
in control, the needle
and the thread ready, but
heart racing, accidents
happen, with sweat dripping
down her brow, worried now
about the potential
for errors, staring at
the thread in one hand, now
heavy compared to the
past feelings, the silver
needle cold against her
sweaty palms, she needed

to relax, flashes of

blood and piercing flesh, or

worse, the patient's eyes ran

in a loop of her mind

sitting the tools down on

the table next to her

she closed her eyes and sat

in silence hoping that

maybe, the young girl so

eager for the perfect

lashes would change her mind

and simply accept her

own natural beauty,

maybe she could avoid

any harm, any sewing

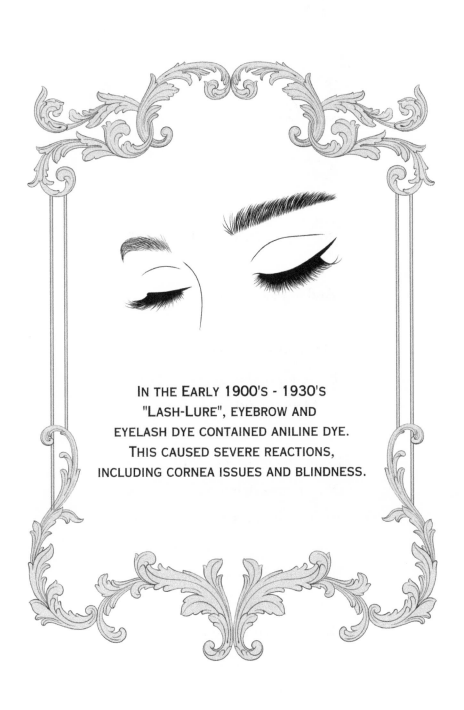

IN THE EARLY 1900's - 1930's
"LASH-LURE", EYEBROW AND
EYELASH DYE CONTAINED ANILINE DYE.
THIS CAUSED SEVERE REACTIONS,
INCLUDING CORNEA ISSUES AND BLINDNESS.

Blind to the Allure

She could hide behind layers of
Makeup, everything polished
And in place, perfect - always.

Though it was never enough,
Each day and night, she craved
More attention - always.

In the salon she chose the allure
Of lash lure, dying her eyelashes
For a dash of more beauty - always.

Days after, eyes swollen and
Oozing, her lids heavy with her
Burden, vanity won - always.

Doctor after doctor, all the same,

Her eyesight gone long after the

Bandages removed, blind - always.

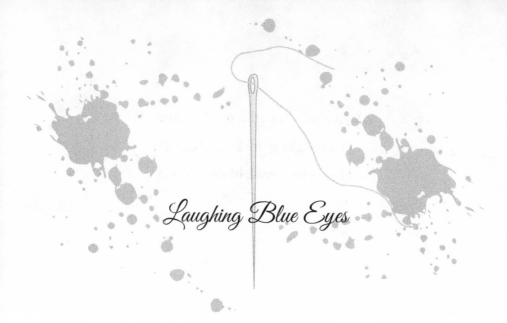

Laughing Blue Eyes

Lure them in, the eligible
Gentlemen, you will grace them with
Your presence and your twinkling smile,
Wow them with your laughing blue eyes.

With your dainty figure and your
elegant clothes, all you needed
was a small splash of color to
radiate your personality.

The salon was stocked, and you were
fully ready to commit to
A slight change in your appearance
new and improved, eyelash dye.

And you, armed with a hot desire
to become the most dazzling
lady in society, with
hauntingly gorgeous eyes, well framed.

But beauty comes at a price and
It was much too steep for you, with
swollen and oozing eyes, closed not
by choice, but out of pain, your eyes

will never be the same, bandaged
up and cleaned by doctors, the dye
still remains in place, but your eyes
hazy and faded, no longer

laughing now, blinded forever.

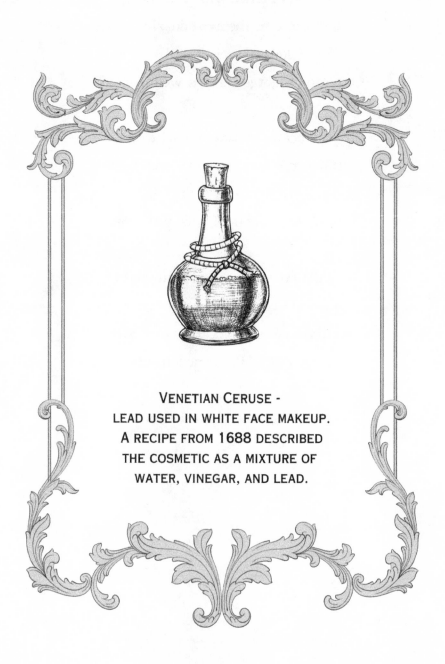

VENETIAN CERUSE -
LEAD USED IN WHITE FACE MAKEUP.
A RECIPE FROM 1688 DESCRIBED
THE COSMETIC AS A MIXTURE OF
WATER, VINEGAR, AND LEAD.

Fashionably Useless

Clasping her hands together
Firmly - as tight as possible.

Her wrists, weak and dainty
In appearance, now useless.

They hung there, while she'd
Always enjoyed others doing

Things for her, this lack of
Independence crushed her.

To be one of the fashionable
Women about town - dressed

In fine silks and face white in
Pallor, she was adored by many.

Though now, waiting for the
Doctor, she was merely a ghost

Of herself, frail and pale, her
Wrists wasted away, pathetic.

Trying to clasp her hands, she
Tried and tried, but her wrists

Limply hanging there, as she
Listened to the doctor explain.

Lead poisoning, her makeup,
It all wove together, the pieces

As tears fell freely, she swore
She'd never wear makeup again.

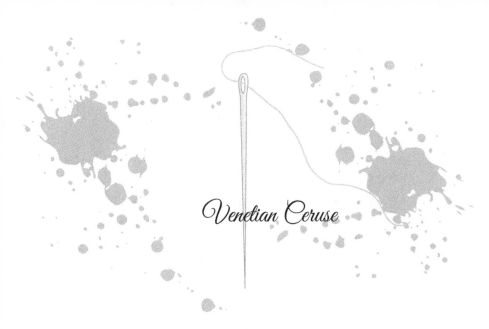

Venetian Ceruse

My family passed down its recipe for
The highly coveted Venetian ceruse,
Our very own makeup, for making
The most fashionable lady in court.

All of the aristocracy came to us
For the little ceramic jars holding
The sacred treasure within, the face
Makeup to smooth out complexions.

For decades my family has passed this
Glorious mix of products down, the key
Is simplicity - water, vinegar, and lead,
Everything you need for beauty in a jar.

With greying hair and faces covered
In pox marks, everyone needed a little
Mystery for their overall appearance
With wigs and makeup, to be complete.

Dry skin and stomach pains aside,
To be the belle of any ball and have
All eyes on you as you dance around
The room with all the eligible suitors.

Your white face the color of death's
Bones, he may knock at your door,
But at least you'll know that you are
Beauty embodied, for all eternity.

A Dash of Lead

Clad in the finest silks and satins
That the seamstresses can acquire,
My entrance into society is all
That anyone can talk about now.

The making of a fashionable lady
Is more than just the dresses and
The jewels that are draped around
Her neck and adorn her hands.

With skin smooth like porcelain,
And complexion as white as a
Freshly fallen snow, these other
Factors make a lady most desirable.

Hiding any spots, any moles, any
And every flaw, the bloom of ninon
Turns any lovely fair lady into a
True beauty, envious to all eyes.

Comprised of almond emulsion,
The essence of lavender, and just
A dash of white lead, this mixture
Goes on evenly, painting the skin.

Ignore the side effects, the grey
Hair comes with age anyways,
And while your skin may be dry,
It will be velvety, soft to the touch.

Blossoming in society, my beauty
And my clothing are both a success,
My stomach pains shrugged off,
As the days pass and suitors line up.

The rubies and little diamonds that
Sparkle along my décolletage are
Nothing compared to my face, for
I am a most fashionable lady.

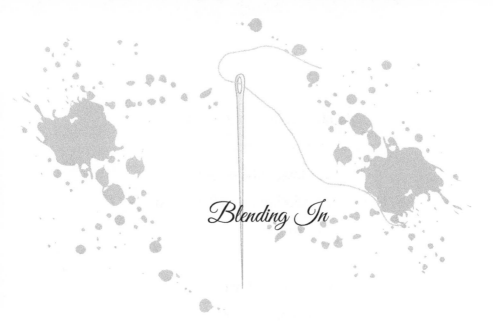

Blending In

The little jar, full of beauty,
Was heavy in her hand, the
Bloom of Youth contained
The richest ingredients to
Turn even a deep tan into

An enviable pallor, and as
A new member of the upper
Class with socialite status,
She needed any and all help
Possible to simply blend
In with the other women.

As she applied the cream
Each and every day, she did
Feel as though she belonged,
Her skin smooth pale as the moon
Dressed in similar gowns.

She was invited for tea and
Attended all the popular
Events in town, she had
Finally begun to feel as if
She was welcomed and all
The thanks were given to

The little lead–laced jar of
Cream, even when her hands
Begun to feel off, and when
She could no longer lift
A teacup for her wrists and

Her hands, delicate, but not working.
She continued to use the cream
Despite what the doctors did
Say, she needed to blend in.

If she died and was buried
Tomorrow it would be no
Surprise to anyone, she was
Already the color of a corpse.

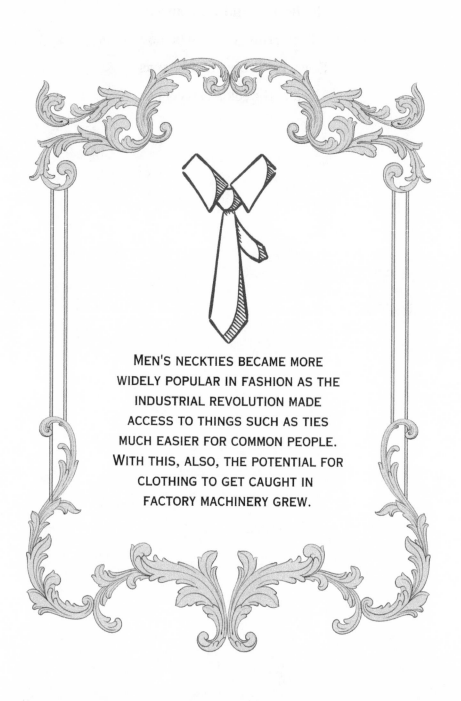

MEN'S NECKTIES BECAME MORE
WIDELY POPULAR IN FASHION AS THE
INDUSTRIAL REVOLUTION MADE
ACCESS TO THINGS SUCH AS TIES
MUCH EASIER FOR COMMON PEOPLE.
WITH THIS, ALSO, THE POTENTIAL FOR
CLOTHING TO GET CAUGHT IN
FACTORY MACHINERY GREW.

Head in the Clouds

Even as he stood, still, staring
At his reflection in the mirror,
He thought about their life
Together, she was his sun.

He'd toil long hours to make
Sure she had the world, just
For that lingering smile of hers.

With everything in place, a
Quick straightening of his tie,
He headed off to the factory.

Each and every day tedious
In this confined place, yet
He remained, working hard.

She had agreed to marry him,
The ring modest, her feelings
Earnest, his head in the clouds.

Moving through the motions,
Mind in a daydream, his tie
Caught in the steel, fear and
Shock coursed through him.

His beloved forced to confirm
The remains of his mess, well
What was left, her heart broken
And her wedding never to be.

Tie In Place

The dusty factory floor
Was louder than usual,
machines ticking and
everything clicking
he closed his eyes
trying to take a deep
breath, much to no avail
the dingy room crowded
his skin felt hot, his head
pounding, loosening his
tie, he headed towards
his station, ready to work
though after a bit he felt
dizzy and he swayed, his
tie, tied in a popular way
the latest *Neckclothitania*

pamphlet had shown, got
caught in the wheel, and
his cotton tie stuck, pulling
him swiftly to his demise.

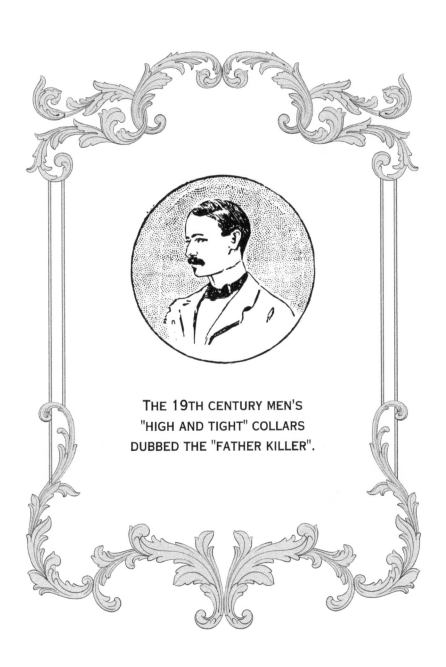

THE 19TH CENTURY MEN'S
"HIGH AND TIGHT" COLLARS
DUBBED THE "FATHER KILLER".

Collar Death

Starched, almost too stiff for comfort,
But very presentable worn over
The freshly pressed men's cotton shirt,
Ready for the day, off he went to work.

Long hours and for long days, he worked
Ever dreaming of that promotion,
Each day he came in dressed his best
Hoping his appearance would impress.

Walking in the park one day, after
Several hours spent in the smoky bar,
And perhaps one too many drinks, though
All in good spirits, he went for a stroll.

Walking in the park, he enjoyed the cool
Breeze and darkness, sitting on a bench,
Tiredness overcame him and, getting
Comfortable he rested his head.

The next day, as the sun shone brightly above,
They discovered his body, cold and stiff,
His ever–fashionable collar blocked off
Breathing, suffocating him in his sleep.

His Only Vice

Detached, his collar and
His mind, the stiffness
Of the fabric, the stiff
Rules he always followed

Tight, too tight perhaps,
The collar buttoned shut

Deep breaths, laughing, even
Singing, all uncomfortable

Lack of fresh air, why not
Cloud it all with his smoke

A lit cigar, his only vice,
Tonight, his cause of death

Detached, they try to help,
Removing the high collar but it's much
Too late, he suffocated, unable
To breathe, finally free.

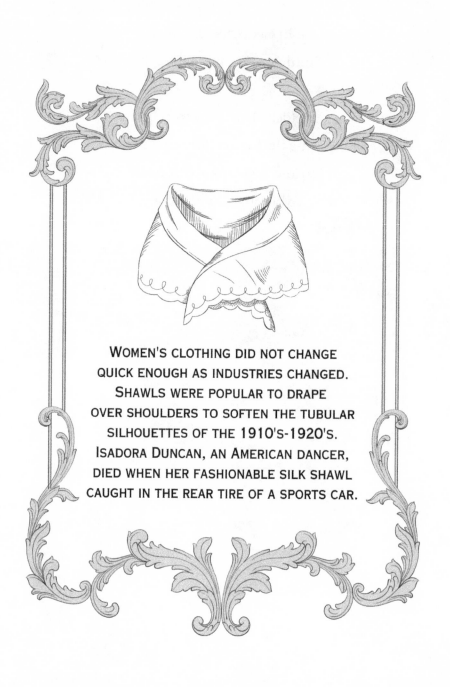

WOMEN'S CLOTHING DID NOT CHANGE
QUICK ENOUGH AS INDUSTRIES CHANGED.
SHAWLS WERE POPULAR TO DRAPE
OVER SHOULDERS TO SOFTEN THE TUBULAR
SILHOUETTES OF THE 1910'S-1920'S.
ISADORA DUNCAN, AN AMERICAN DANCER,
DIED WHEN HER FASHIONABLE SILK SHAWL
CAUGHT IN THE REAR TIRE OF A SPORTS CAR.

Isadora's Shawl

Painted delicately,
And handled just the
Same, she wrapped her long
And elegant silk shawl
Around her shoulders,
And around her neck.

Isadora went out
Her hips and her legs
Moving gracefully
All eyes were always on
Her, and with that, her
Appearance her world.

Waving to the small crowd
Gathered near the swell
Amilcar sports car.
She took the backseat, her
Driver, so dashing,
With a smile she wrapped

Her scarf about her neck,
Looping and looping,
She smiled, all ready
To go, and as the car
Sped away, her smile
Always bright, faded

Unable to stop it,
The silk shawl, dainty
In look, got caught in
The tire, unable to
Scream, it happened so
Quickly, and in mere

Minutes Isadora
Was dead, strangled to death
By her favorite
Accessory, even
In death, her fashion
Taste was exquisite.

Draped in Silk and Blood

Hand-painted silk went
With everything and
Felt lovely against
Her skin, true beauty
Came from within, but
When the shawl was draped
Around her shoulders
She felt stunning, so
Irresistible,
She could not wait to
Show it off, each night
And day, she'd wear it.

Always in style and
Always so gorgeous
Galivanting, all

Across town with her
Potential suitors
All wanting her hand
And her future, one
Night, too quick to leave
She draped the silk shawl
Snug around her neck
And shoulders for warmth
And as the door shut
Her future was set
In stone, and when they
Drove away she gasped
Sharply death was here.

Just mere seconds had
Passed, for as the car
Stopped, her neck had snapped
And as the blood dripped
From her eyes and nose
Her delicate features
Stained, her body draped
In silk and blood as
She took her final breath.

"RADIUM GIRLS," CONTRACTED
RADIATION POISONING FROM THE
MAKING OF POPULAR WATCHES.

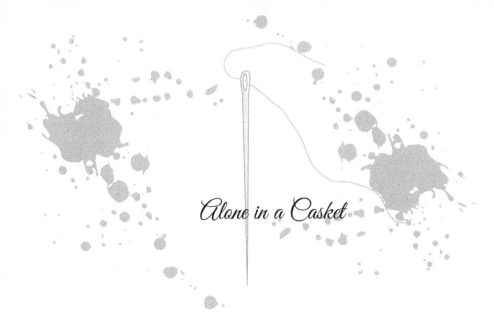

Alone in a Casket

Glowing, dimly in the

Twilight, the moon making

It's way into the sky,

The cold darkness enveloping

Her body, its effervescent-like

Glint noticeable with each

And every passing moment

As the sun set on the horizon,

Her head became dizzy

The jaw pain, the toothaches,

The unsettling nausea

It all made sense now

Staring at her hands,

The green tint to her nails

Too much to take in now

Her mother had joked months
Ago about how painting those
Silly little fashionable watches
Would be the death of her,
Little did they know that those
Words were heavy with truth,
Her heart sank, thinking of all
The girls who had gone
Homesick only to never
Return to work again, her
Name would join theirs in
The newspaper - chronicling
The deaths of every community
Member, her family would
Mourn their loss and her corpse
Would glow, alone in a casket
Until decaying completely.

Precious Radiant Time

Dip, lick, paint, the time passes by
Swiftly, as we work our days away.
The precise watch dials in the ever
So fashionable self-luminous paint.

One of the girls discovered her nails
Would glow hours later, without polish
And another noticed her skin, once pale
Had a little glowing tint to it at night.

Dip, lick, paint, the days pass by us,
We giggle and gossip, eager to see
Whose dress would glimmer, and be
Radiant after we left the factory.

Weeks went by with nothing new,
Though a girl or two complained
With aches, both tooth and jaw,
And were out sick, worry took over.

Dip, lick, paint, time is precious,
Every moment here means a minute
Less spent out there, with family and
Friends, we watch the ghost girls dim.

The paint is poison, though not every
Girl is sick and the courthouse fights
Make everyone involved, the factory
Silent as the watch hands tick us by.

Dip, lick, paint, there are so few of us
Left now, dedicating painting watches,
The images of the dead girls are forever
Ingrained in my mind, fear envelops me.

My teeth, my bones, my entire being
Feels frail now, and my time, ticking by
Quickly, spent in a hospital as my jaw
Decays, soon I'll take my last breath.

Firefly Like Glow

She little down at her fingers,
Her nails were glowing, just a tad
In the darkness of her kitchen,
She wiggled her fingers, seeing if
Maybe the moonlight streaming in
The window was the root cause of the
Little flickering lights, like fireflies
Dancing along with her movements,
But it was just her nails, just her.

So peculiar she thought, moving
Her fingers slowly, wondering how
It came about, this odd glowing.

As a working girl, she had little time
To spend worrying about these things,

Once at work, surrounded by the
Other girls, painting the wristwatches,
She felt at ease as they chatted about
How their nails - or their teeth or their
Dresses - glimmered at home as well.

Comforted by these experiences
She continued on, gently licking the
Brush, dipping it into the powder, her
Brushwork perfected over time, the
Pieces completed were exquisite,
Or so she thought, and as the days passed
She forgot about the odd glowing
All of the girls had encountered, until
One by one, the room once full of joy and
Laughter had become eerily empty.

The charming watches, still popular, sat
Unfinished, until the girls were replaced.

Room Full of Ghost Girls

Looking forward to work, with a
Spring in her step, she was eager
To get to painting the delicate and
Elegant watches, the time passed
Quickly at work, her job required
A lot of concentration and effort.

She longed to one day be manager,
Or something more than just another
Of the painters, all of the girls
Lined up in a row, dipping their
Brushes - almost in sync - as
The clock ticked by, the room always
Silent as all the girls worked the
Day away, carefully painting all
Of the popular, stylish watches.

As the seasons changed, some of the
Girls became ill, little fatigue
And a touch of nausea, though for others
They experienced severe pain,
From toothaches to ulcers, the
Room once full of girls began to dwindle.

Until only a few of them were left,
Still painting the captivating watches,
Movements slow, each radiant
Girl now a shadow of herself, it
Was too late for all of them, their
Bodies too exposed to the radium
Dust in the paint, they had all
Ingested from their perfected method
Of dipping their wet brushes, the watches

Would continue to tick and sell, but
These ghost girls would fade away
As time passed, their lives were cast aside.

IN THE 19TH CENTURY, IT WAS
POPULAR TO HAVE AN HOURGLASS SHAPE
WITH A WAIST THAT WAS
NO MORE THAN 21 INCHES.
CORSETRY WAS USED AND A MYTH
THAT RIBS WERE REMOVED TO ACHIEVE
AN EVEN SMALLER WAIST.

Sinful Desires

The fabric pushed against
My bare skin, my cotton
Chemise cold, dampened with
Sweat, it clings to me, the
Corset is laced, pulling
The laces tight until
Everything is in place.

With short breaths and long skirts
Everything in place now
The silk sways as I move
About the room, dizzy
And lightheaded, but still
I mingle, hopeful for
A suitor's interest.

Though truthfully, as I
Mill about, my thoughts and
Daydreams are full of deep
Breaths, unrestricted and
Running through the tall grass
Until I'm standing at
The ocean's edge, now free.

The salty air filling
My lungs as I breathe in the
Crisp air, my most sinful desire.

It will never happen,
Forever locked inside
The birdcage, my corset
Tightened each day until
I die, my organs now
Permanently shifted.

Perhaps with my dying breath
I'll be able to fill
My lungs, a desire
Buried with me.

Laced and Sinched

Deep breaths and admiring
The ocean's waves and salty air
Were reserved for the working
Class women, for those refined
Ladies within high society were
Limited with their breaths.

Confined to corsets - laced and
Sinched as tight as possible - they
Could never relax or enjoy the
Fresh air that would never quite
Fill their lungs, constrained in the
Corsetry that held them together.

Underneath layers - and layers - of
Silk and satin gowns, the boning held
Everything in place, providing the
Ever unattainable tiny waist, making
These women the most desirable.

It was never enough for the delicate
Ladies - or for the society - they
Needed smaller and smaller waists.

Some dared to think outside - or
rather inside - the box and pursued
The removal of several of their ribs.

Giving them an even smaller, more
Elusive and fragile appearance,
All to land a well–to–do suitor and
Secure a happily ever after in this
Most fashionable and sad city.

Dire Choices

As a lady with merit, with grace,
She needed to mold herself to the
Standards set by high society,
For she needed to be elegant and
Fashionable, she needed more.

As she lay in bed, the covers
Pulled up tight and the fire
Roaring, keeping her warm
In this frightening night, she
Doubted her earlier actions.

Stitches and bandages and pain
Were all she had now, unable
To leave her bed for anything,
Needing help to move about,
Unable to relax, her mind torn.

Corsetry was the leading style,
The smaller the waist the better,
And finding it hard to achieve
Any better result, she had turned
To dire choices, and surgery.

Without a few ribs, she could
Have that dainty little waist
That all the other girls would
Envy, she'd be the center of
Attention at each societal event.

Though, now with complications,
She faced days and nights spent
Alone and in bed, her body angry
And trying to fight the infection
That threatened her with Death
Becoming her suitor this season.

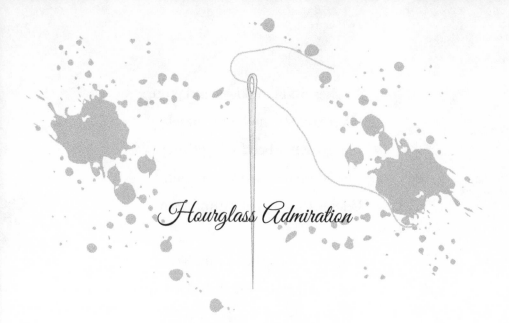

Hourglass Admiration

The standard of beauty, the
Height of fashion is found
Within a woman's silhouette,
Not what lies beneath, within
Her self, just the gown's look.

Boning, from top to bottom,
Held their stomachs in place,
The corsets becoming tighter
And tighter as the seasons
Changed, the hourglass figure
The epitome of elegance now.

You could feel the changes
Happening within your body,
Things felt out of place, and

Perhaps it was organs, moving
About, creating new homes for
Themselves in your body, you
Strived for that delicate waist.

Feeling lightheaded, but you
Still carry on with the corsetry
And the tightlacing, yet none
Of it matters, your waist is still
Not small enough in your eyes.

With fainting spells and a bit
Of unease when moving too
Much, especially anything more
Then a simple walk, you make
A rash decision, something that
Would change your livelihood.

As you lie on the table, the cold
Steel chilling your exposed skin,
You take your last deep breaths,
Something you haven't been able
To do in quite some time, when
You wake you'll feel lighter and
Tinnier, without a few ribs though.

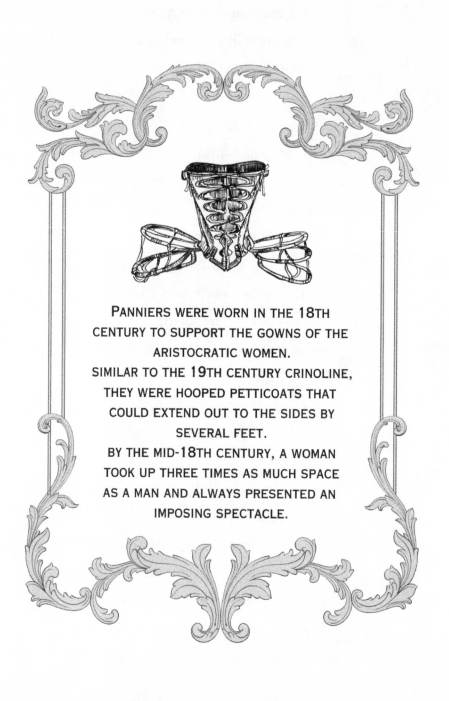

PANNIERS WERE WORN IN THE 18TH
CENTURY TO SUPPORT THE GOWNS OF THE
ARISTOCRATIC WOMEN.
SIMILAR TO THE 19TH CENTURY CRINOLINE,
THEY WERE HOOPED PETTICOATS THAT
COULD EXTEND OUT TO THE SIDES BY
SEVERAL FEET.
BY THE MID-18TH CENTURY, A WOMAN
TOOK UP THREE TIMES AS MUCH SPACE
AS A MAN AND ALWAYS PRESENTED AN
IMPOSING SPECTACLE.

Penelope's Panniers

As she stood there, Penelope
Was frozen in place, how could
Something so grisly like this ever
Happen to someone like her, an

Aristocrat, a member of the court,
Someone who wore the finest of
Silks and always had jewels to
Match, but as the fire raged on

In the small sitting room, she
Couldn't leave, her wide panniers
Though sturdy and fashionable,
Had kept her stuck there, unable

To leave, and as the flames got
Closer - and closer - and the room
Filled with smoke, she could smell
The fabrics start to burn and all

Of her screams were lost among
The roaring fire, she eventually
Lost consciousness, her panniers
A stark contrast to the ash and

Charred remains left behind, the
Last thing anyone would say is
That they were jealous of Penelope
And her lovely taste in gowns

Despite the death and debris left,
No other lady in court could bare
To leave their home without their
Trusty panniers, wide as ever.

Gilt Lace and Burnt Maze

From many hours of practicing,

With her lady-in-waiting by

Her side – she was eager to test

Out her dancing skills in her new

Silken gown, heavy with jewels

Draped upon her, the embroidered

Dress burdensome on her dainty

Frame, with muscles barely there she

Relied on whalebone panniers

To hold the weight of the gown from

Pulling her to the ground.

Silver thread caught glimmers of the
Warm evening sun as she strolled from
The carriage to the ballroom, the
Gilt lace sewn on her cream skirting
Opulent – just like the rubies
Hanging from her ears and those
At her throat – her status,
No introduction needed.

As the evening wore on, laughter
And music filled the halls, voices
Echoed amongst the marble walls
She sought silence, wandering to
The gardens, the maze offering
Peace and quiet from the social
Requirements, as she sat on a
Bench admiring a fountain, she
Closed her eyes, briefly asleep, when
Smoke filled her nostrils she awoke
Amongst flames, the hedges on fire
All around her, no clear way out
She tried to move, but her body
Was too tired from dancing, too frail
From her refined life, the paniers
Held her dress up, but blocked her path

Unable to use any small
Opening that appeared through the
Blaze, she would die here, the yards of
Fabric holding her down,
Melting to her skin as she burned.

IN THE 19TH CENTURY
BALLERINA TUTUS WERE MADE WITH
TULLE, WHICH WERE OFTEN LAYERED
AND STIFFENED WITH STARCH. THIS
PROCESS ADDED TO THE FLAMMABILITY
OF THE SKIRTS. WITH CANDLE LIGHTING IN
THEATERS, MANY BALLERINAS SUFFERED
BURNS OR DEATH FROM FIRES.

Twirling in Tulle

Around and around
They twirl
Their slender silhouettes
Casting elegant shadows
Against the hand-painted backdrops
As the flames flicker from the front

The glow against the dancers
Clad in tulle skirts and not much
Else, the girls continue to
Pirouette and leap across
The stage to the music and
The admiration of the crowd

Until the screams of a ballerina
Echo sharply throughout the theater
And the crowd shouts for water
As the smoke billows throughout

Around and around
She twirls
Trying to put the fire out
As the tulle, and her skin, melts

Burned to a crisp
The newspapers will write
But still, everyone will come
To the next show,
The dead easily replaced.

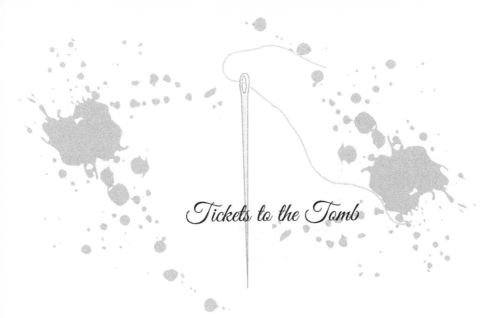

Tickets to the Tomb

all the dancers milled about
stretching and practicing the
show was just hours away now

all clad in the crisp, white skirts
and matching bodices, the
ballerinas sparkled on
stage as the curtains went up

their legs, exposed against the
firm skirts, the layers of tulle
highlighting their tiny waists.

dancing about the stage, each
girl elegant en pointe, like
ethereal beings they
pirouette gracefully

engrossed in the music and
the dancing, one exquisite
ballerina got too close

a slight touch, and in a blink,
smoke and flames engulfed her, as
the dancer spun about, the
fire consumed her tulle, and her.

despite the horror and grim
reminder, the theater
continued on the next day

despite whispers and gossip,
the people still came, with their
tickets to the gaslit theater,
but would they see a ballet,

or would they take a trip to the tomb?

19TH CENTURY WOMEN'S CRINOLINE HOOP
SKIRTS WERE NOT ONLY A FIRE HAZARD,
THEY WOULD GET CAUGHT IN
MACHINERY AND CARRIAGE WHEELS.
GUSTS OF WIND AND OTHER OBSTACLES
PROVED PROBLEMATIC.

Charred Crinoline

Inspired by the details of Henry Wadsworth Longfellow's wife's death in 1861.

It provided structure, a lovely
And enhanced silhouette for every
Lady in society, the crinoline skirt
Was stiff beneath all the fabric layers.

Sitting in the library, she carried on
Her tasks, nothing was ever easy in
A crinoline, nothing too comfortable,
She hummed as she worked on seals.

It only took a brief moment, not even
Enough to gasp, when something
Maybe a match - or a piece of paper
That had caught fire - fell on her lap.

The crinoline, providing the desirable
Look, was much too flammable, her
Entire skirt caught fire, the beautiful
Flames soon engulfed her completely.

Smoke filled her lungs, her nose
Unable to wrinkle at the melting skin
That was blistering and peeling off,
Her voice gone, it happened too fast.

Bedridden and unable to heal, the doctor
Proclaimed they spend the last few
Moments they had together, and she
Accept her fate, her husband distraught.

The final moments, her final breaths,
Were full of sweet murmurs from her
Devoted husband, trying to cover up
The children's cries, she closed her eyes.
Another woman - another death - gone
Up in flames, in only a day she had
Lost her life, from a little spark her
Crinoline, her fancy attire, her demise.

Up in Flames

The steel cage hoops gave Joan
The ability to have the most dazzling
Of skirt silhouettes, she would be
The belle of any social gathering
This spring, she would dazzle and
Sparkle like a diamond in the sea
Of ladies dressed in satins spinning
About the dance floor, and hopefully
Joan would catch a suitor's eye,
She wanted to fall in love and she
Dreamed of a wedding full of tulips
And the finest silk gown she would
Ever touch with her hands, Joan was
Daydreaming again, her mind just
Wandering as she longed for her
Dreams to come true, for love and

Laughter and children to be her
Future and as Joan finished getting
Ready for the big evening event,
She pulled her lace gloves on,
And as stood by the fireplace, the
Flames roaring, keeping the home
Warm this chilly spring evening,
She looked out the window, waiting
For her carriage to arrive to take her
Off to the dance, where she longed
To meet a lovely suitor, daydreaming
Of a dance and a kiss and romance,
She was lost in her head as the smoke
Billowed around her, and it was too late
For she was all alone by the fireplace
As her crinoline went up in flames, and
Poor Joan died along with her dreams.

Seaside Social Strolls

Afternoons strolls, a daily dose of
Sunshine and social time, was a
Part of everyday life for those
Living in the quaint, coastal town.

All the ladies - from high society
Down to simple maids - had the
Latest steel–caged hoop skirts
Under their voluminous gowns.

Bows adorned the satins and silks,
Their outfits weren't quite complete
Without gloves, capelets, and perhaps
Even a bonnet adorning their curls.

Though, as the time went on, and
The chances of stormy weather
Rolled in, the ladies simply went
About their daily lives, strolls too.

One day, a cluster of well dressed
Women walked along the cliffside,
Ignoring the grey clouds and winds
Coming in quickly, they continued.

The steel cage hoops held their skirts
Well, but as the wind grew stronger,
And stronger, the ladies tried their
Best to keep their feet on the ground.

One by one, the lovely ladies, adorned
With bows, accessories and social status
Were swept up by the gusty winds and
Thrown over the cliffside, into the sea.

The crinoline skirts were soon much
Too heavy for these dainty ladies, the
Storm too loud above muffling all their
Salty screams, one by one they drowned.

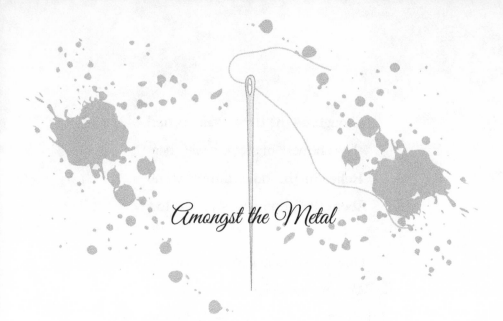

Amongst the Metal

She had finally saved enough
Money to spend on the latest
A steel-caged crinoline.

The perfect piece to accentuate
Her waist and silhouette.

Gently smoothing her skirt
Making sure everything was in
Place, she headed out to work.

Amid the dust and the noise,
She toiled away at the factory
Among a sea of women.

Despite the weight, she was
Happy to have her new crinoline.

As she moved to take a moment,
Brief as it was, to sit and rest,
A horrifying thing occurred.

Her skirt caught in the mechanical
Press, pulling her body into it.

Nothing could be done, she was
Lost amongst the metal, between
The crinoline and the machines.

Welcome the Silence

Living in bustling city was exciting
For her, she longed for the morning
Strolls, seeing all the stores opening
And all of the people rushing to and
From homes and work, eager for the
Day to start and for life to carry on.

Chatter and squeals of delight from
Children, her ears and mind bounced
Around from everything going on
Around her as she made her way
Through the streets, her eyes darting
All around, her senses overwhelmed,

As a little country mouse, the city
Was a lot to take in - the smells,
The yelling, the sheer number of
People everywhere - but she reveled
In these morning strolls when the sun
Was just right and a tad magical.

One day, like any other ordinary one,
She went out for a stroll, her crinoline
And dress in order, parasol ready to go,
She wandered down the road, heading
To cross the street, her eyes closed, the
Desire to relish this moment an error.

As her skirts silently glided along the
Road, the wheels of carriage came by
And ran over the bottom, catching her
Crinoline and with it, taking her down
And as the back wheels rolled over her
Body, her senses overwhelmed again.

Ladies nearby shrieking, children were
Screaming, she had heard what must've
Been bones cracking, the crimson red
Blood covered everything she saw, and

She wasn't sure if the sun beaming was
Keeping her warm, but the hand that she
Took was ice cold, and then she closed
Her eyes, welcoming the silence.

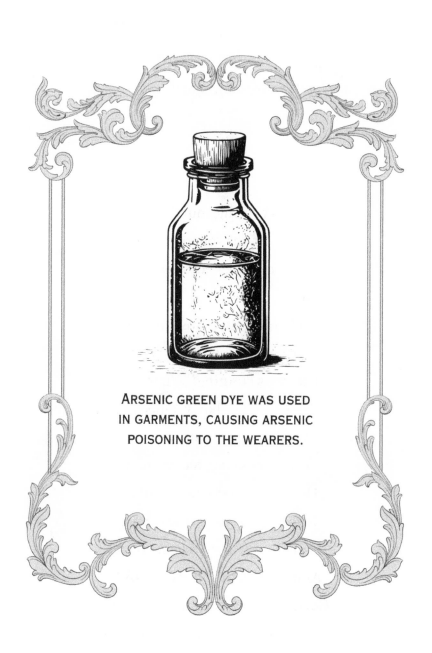

ARSENIC GREEN DYE WAS USED
IN GARMENTS, CAUSING ARSENIC
POISONING TO THE WEARERS.

Immaculate but Green

Heart racing, thundering
In her chest, the sound practically
Screaming in her ears, her breath
Caught, as her mind – scattered
And uncertain – was running
Around, or was it her body
That was running? What was
Happening, her hands smoothed
Over her skirts, palms sweaty,
The room much too hot, and
Her vision – once immaculate
Like herself – was tinted, now
Everything tinged a light green
Almost matching her beautiful
Gown she had worn to this event,
Almost. Almost. Almost.

Dizzy and uneasy, she sought
A couch to relax, as this passed
She hoped it would pass,
In the quiet confines
Of this darkened room,
She closed her eyes and
Took a deep breath, though
Slightly difficult, yet her last.

Your Dance with Death

You needed the very best, hand-sewn

Dresses, with delicate lace and lovely

Bows adorning the bodice. Your skirts

Had volume and your shoes matched

Your headdress oh so perfectly.

And while your suitor was dressed

Equally as handsomely, you didn't know

That real suitor that evening, the highlight

Of the social season, the moment seared

In your mind, would be the dance with Death.

You knew the waltz by heart, the rhythm
In tune with your heartbeat as you moved
So gracefully about the dancefloor, with
Your green skirts swirling around, your hand
In his, as Death soon took the lead.

The whites of your eyes now green in hue,
The feeling of anxiety creeping through your bones,
You waltzed and waltzed around the floor,
With Death staring through your soul, his hands
Keeping you steady as your muscles convulsed.

You waltzed and waltzed until everything
Was green in hue, the crowd seemed far away,
And every single breath you took ragged,
Looking at your hand in his, you couldn't tell
If it was a trick or if your nails were truly emerald.

As Death led you from the floor, you vomited
Not from the dizzying dance, but from the arsenic
Used to tint your stunning evening gown, that made
You the true belle of the ball, but was it all worth it?
For your last dance to be with Death.

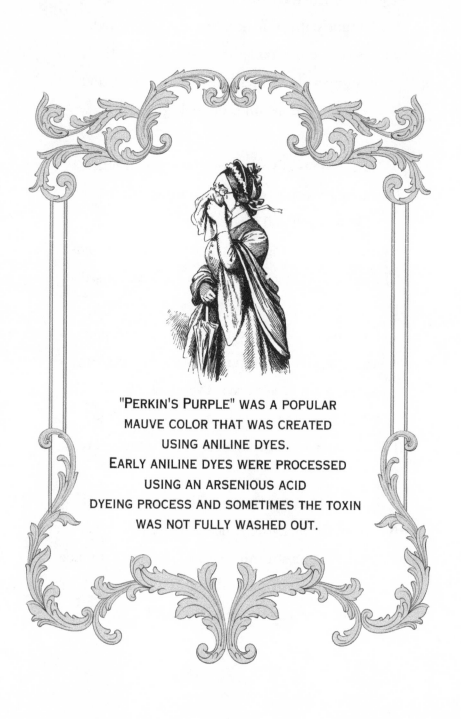

"PERKIN'S PURPLE" WAS A POPULAR
MAUVE COLOR THAT WAS CREATED
USING ANILINE DYES.
EARLY ANILINE DYES WERE PROCESSED
USING AN ARSENIOUS ACID
DYEING PROCESS AND SOMETIMES THE TOXIN
WAS NOT FULLY WASHED OUT.

Maladies in Mauve

With her head in the clouds,
Daydreaming of all the
Lovely fabrics - the satins
And silks - and how they
Would feel against her skin,
She desired a closet busting
At the seams of her wardrobe,
Wanting the lace and delicate
Embroidered dresses and
Blouses to adorn her dainty
Body, from head to toe, she'd
Dress her best, with the most
Fashionable colors she'd prance
About town, in mauve or
Magenta, she was the shining
Diamond against the dreary

Wools and cottons, she loved
Her colorful dyed clothing,
The purples always her favorite,
And even after falling ill,
Adamant to continue dressing
Stylish, despite being confined
To bed, her skin covered in rashes
Her face flushed with fever
And dress soaked with sweat,
She'd rather die before she wore
Something plain, and so as the
Beautiful, Perkin's purple dye
Continued to seep into her bones,
She'd be buried, her malady
Too much for her body, enclosed
In her casket, surrounded by her
Favorite gowns, she would decay.

Even in Death

the color fresh and new,

exactly what she needed

to win the eye of a suitor

the dresses in mauve or

magenta, the silk crisp as

she dressed, appearance everything

the blues and reds, all old

and outdated, she sparkled

in the waves of socialites

waltzing and mingling she

made her way around the room

eager for romance, heart racing

like a diamond among

pearls, she shined brightly tonight,

her beauty both inside and out

the next day, weary and
tired, she remained in bed, her
weak body aching, feverish

flowers from suitor lined
the room, the curtains pulled shut,
the darkness hiding her rashes
her mind gave in to the
fever dreams, as her suitor,
the love of her life was here - Death
arrived, her frail body
restless now as her pale arms
outstretched, welcoming him to her

with her final breath, her body
sagged, and the mourners cried tears
as she was buried in

her favorite silk dress,
the magenta bright, her corpse
would dazzle, even after death

IN THE LATE 1800'S AND EARLY 1900'S
THE FLANNELETTE FABRIC WAS
HIGHLY POPULAR AS WELL AS
HIGHLY COMBUSTIBLE.

All Consuming

Clad in flannelette - the family
Slept comfortably, far away in
Dreamland when parents awoke

The screaming cries for help,
Too soft against the crackling
Of the flames consuming all.

A home full of laughter and love
And children means nothing now.

Fire consumes everything in its
Path, it takes no cries of mercy
Into consideration, it devours.

When firefighters arrived and the
Home lay in smoke and ashes,
The children buried in ruble, their
Clothing melted to the bones.

Yearning for Warmth

The candles were lit, and the
Fireplace was roaring, shivering
Ever so slightly, her skin had
Goosebumps, the thin flannelette
Nightgown provided little warmth,
She yearned for the comforting
And snuggling wool pieces she
Had been so used to wearing,
But as their status changed, so
Too did their everyday items,
And for now, she would go with
The flow of this newfound upper
Class system she had fallen into.

The clock struck, the evening

Passing her by, she got up to

Start blowing all the candles

Out, but stumbled on the hem

Of her nightgown, and as she

Threw her arms out to brace

Herself, she knocked a candle

Down and all it took was a

Little flame, and her gown

Ignited, overwhelming her

Entire being, everything on

Fire and smoke filled the room

As the flannelette melted along

With her skin, agony and pain

Were the last feelings she

Experienced in this lifetime.

Melted Dreams

Dressed in his evening attire,
The latest purchase his wife
Had made, a soft flannelette
Nightshirt and thicker wool
Socks, he was ready to sleep.

No need for counting sheep,
He was dreaming, his heart full,
When panic swept over, sweat
Coated his skin, fearing his life,
Eyes closed, his body on fire.

He had never been a crier,
But the pain was like a knife,
Stabbing everywhere, and yet
He couldn't wake, room full

Of smoke now, but not a peep

To be heard. The tug of sleep
Had been too strong to pull
Him from his dreams, the threat
Of death as his screams rife
With pain, his bed now a pyre.

He wasn't known as a liar,
But a sound sleeper, his wife
Now a weeping widow, met
No one else, always tearful,
Dreams melted, none to keep.

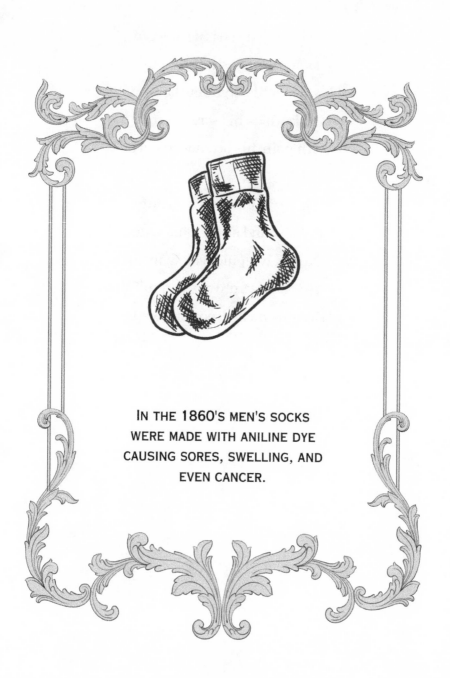

IN THE **1860**'S MEN'S SOCKS
WERE MADE WITH ANILINE DYE
CAUSING SORES, SWELLING, AND
EVEN CANCER.

Colorful Secret

Unwrapping the gift from his beloved,
He held a pair of wool socks, soft
Against his callused hands, the color
A bright and vibrant magenta.

How peculiar he thought, but looking
At his love's smiling face, he held
Them against his chest, promising
Her that he'd wear them all the time.

The socks, though colorful and flashy,
Were hidden under his trousers and
Inside his boots, a secret for just him.

The socks were a thoughtful gift from
His darling, but they seemed a tad
Uncomfortable, despite the softness.

The socks, though he treasured them,
Started to feel odd - or was it his feet
Causing him pain - and he needed rest.

Sitting on the edge of the dresser, the
Socks remained for days, as he was now
Bedridden, his feet swollen and covered
In sores that caused him pain with every

Little ounce of pressure put on them,
He looked at the colorful pair of socks,
The culprit of his pain, and his demise,
But for her sake the secret would remain.

Poisonous Hosiery

poisonous to the touch

as time creeps along

so too does the poison

as it mixes with the

beads of sweat and as

the day goes on and

the sweltering heat

affects your body, the

toxic aniline dye seeps

silently into your system

until your swollen feet,

heavy now and tender

to the touch, the sores

exposed and oozing,

your flashy mauve socks
the source of such
discomfort and pain,

resigned to bedrest
until the surgeon
determines if your feet
will remain attached
to you or not.

IN THE 19TH CENTURY
WOMEN'S HIGH HEELS AND CORSET
MADE WOMEN WALK ODDLY,
DUBBED "THE GRECIAN BEND".

Bent Beauty

Cautious in every
Moment of her life
Breath held

Waist cinched, skirts
Piled high - bustle in
Place - and dainty feet
Teetering in high heels

Chest out, head high.
Breath held.

Picture perfect posture
Bent and hesitant, she
Walks in her heels,
Elegant and in pain.

Chest out, head high.

With a brief wind, she
Falters, balance unstable,
Falling, she tries to brace
Herself to no avail.

Cold pavement against
Her face, body sore.

Her head throbs, the
Pain once sudden, now
Dissipates and slowly
Her breathing fades.

Until she's taken her
Last breath.

Teeter in Society

on her feet she teetered
slow steps she took
an imaginary book
poised on top of her head
breathing in, her corset
snug against her ribs, tight
and hard to breathe, quite
certain she would faint

her heels uncomfortable,
there'd be no surprise
if when removed, cries
of pain released and blood
pooled in her satin shoes
but she needed to go on
and wear the heels, don

any and all fashion trends

as a lady, she truly had
it all, from skin like milk
to wearing the finest silk
garments, so as the blood
seeped through the shoes,
and her posture winding,
clothing and shoes binding
her pain numbing, the heels

would be her demise,
she'd never leave home
a recluse, never to roam
or mingle in society
for as Cinderella lost her
glass slipper, full of fear
and eyes streaming tears
she knew she'd loose toes

unable to teeter on the heels
no longer a lady in society

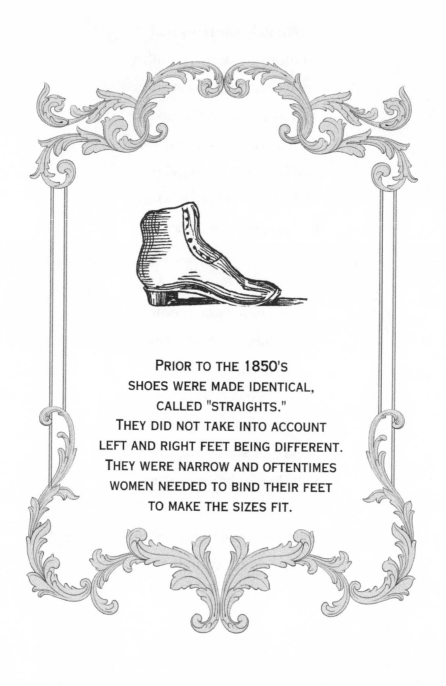

PRIOR TO THE 1850's
SHOES WERE MADE IDENTICAL,
CALLED "STRAIGHTS."
THEY DID NOT TAKE INTO ACCOUNT
LEFT AND RIGHT FEET BEING DIFFERENT.
THEY WERE NARROW AND OFTENTIMES
WOMEN NEEDED TO BIND THEIR FEET
TO MAKE THE SIZES FIT.

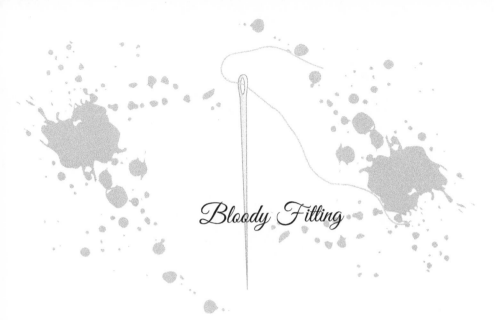

Bloody Fitting

deformed, her feet wide and

uncomfortable in

new satin slippers, the

shoemakers only made

straights, where both her feet – both

shoes – made identical

despite many human

differences. in pain

and with blood, she tried to

fit her feet into these

narrow creations, adorned

with bows and delicate

embroidery though they

would never work – without

a loss of a toe,

or two toes perhaps

Fashion Not Function

Wrapped up tight

My feet are true sights

Of horror, my toes peeping

Just past the bandages

Soaked in sweat and

Tinged with blood

My widened feet unable

To gracefully fit – to

Perfectly slip - into the

Narrow satin straights

That society deems suitable

So, each day, as I breathe

In agony and take tiny

Steps my body aches

In pain, relief only comes
When I sleep, the daytime
Now reserved for my
Nightmares.

About the Author

Brianna Malotke is a member of the Horror Writers Association and an avid coffee drinker. You can find her recent horror work in the anthologies *The Dire Circle, Under Her Skin, Their Ghoulish Reputation, Out of Time, Holiday Leftovers,* and *Horror.Scope*. As far as love and romance go, she has numerous pieces in the anthologies *Worlds Apart, Out of Time, At First Glance, Balm, Tempest,* and *Cherish*. Her debut poetry collection, *Don't Cry on Cashmere,* was published with Ravens Quoth Press in 2022. Looking to fall 2023, her debut romance novella, *Gingerbread Hearts,* will be released with Last Chapter Press. It's the first book in her Sugar & Steam series written under the pen name Tori Fields. For more, visit malotkewrites.com.

Printed in the USA
CPSIA information can be obtained
at www.ICGtesting.com
LVHW051514090823
754555LV00007B/417